Willow Alone

Claire F. Smith

It is summer and weaning time. The best lambs are selected as flock replacements and taken to lowland pasture. Here they call for their mothers until they are hoarse.

The ewes, in contrast, are not so upset. Why should they worry? Weren't they weaned to pasture when they were lambs? They are a family and will welcome their young offspring back into the flock the following spring.

Willow had lived on the hillside with her mother since she was born one sunny spring day in early April.

Now it was summer and she knew where to find water, shelter and things to eat such as tender young grass shoots and wild herbs.

The shepherd knew that the lambs could look after themselves now so it was time to wean them off their mothers' milk. It was also time for their mothers to have a rest before autumn came. So he and his dog Mist set off to gather the sheep from the hill and take them to the pens down in the valley.

Willow had been to the pens before when her mother was sheared and now she tried to stay as close to her as she could.

But the gate closed behind her mother. She followed the other ewes to the left while Willow was carried along with the lambs to the right.

In no time at all Willow found herself in a sheep trailer with the rest of the lambs that had been weaned.

There were slits along the sides of the trailer which let in air and allowed the lambs to look out.

As the trailer moved along everything looked so different to Willow. The hillside faded into the distance and instead Willow saw trees and buildings.

Willow could not SEE her mother.

Everything smelled different.

The damp hill and heather smells were gone and in their place were rich hedgerow and meadow scents.

Willow could not SMELL her mother

Everything sounded different.

Instead of the *pee-wit* of the lapwing she heard the *chack-chack* of the magpie.

Willow could not HEAR her mother.

By the time Willow was let out of the trailer into a tree-filled meadow she was feeling quite lonely.

She called for her mother "*milaaiiir*" as loudly as she could. All the lambs with her were calling out as well so you can imagine that it was very noisy indeed.

Only the trees heard the lambs call.

"Sssh..." they said together, for trees, if they talk at all, usually talk at the same time and almost always in whispers.

“But I’m lonely and sad,” wailed Willow to a nearby plum tree.

The plum tree was called Victoria, a very popular name for plum trees.

Victoria was very old, very wise and she always spoke alone.

"You shouldn't be lonely," said Victoria. "All your friends are here in this meadow. You mustn't feel sad because you will return to the hillside."

"When?" asked Willow feeling more cheerful.

"You will return to the hillside next spring," explained Victoria. "Before that comes autumn when I let the plums on my branches fall down for you to eat."

As Victoria spoke, Willow began to relax in her new home. She looked forward to days eating the good green grass and playing with her lamb friends. Willow knew that Victoria was going to be a very special friend and curled up feeling contented and safe at her roots.

Victoria looked down and saw that Willow had fallen fast asleep. Kindly Victoria spread her leaves to shade Willow from the hot summer sun.

Autumn came. Willow had become so plump eating all the plums, blackberries and grass she was almost as fat as a mole.

She could not have got so FAT on the hillside.

The trees shed their leaves. Victoria didn't wear leaves in the winter as they would hold the snow and the weight would snap her branches. Even without leaves the trees made the meadow very sheltered. So instead of using up her fat to keep warm, Willow could use it to grow bigger.

She could not have grown so BIG on the hillside.

At last the days lengthened and became warmer. Willow could balance on her hind legs to admire Victoria's new leaves. Victoria even let Willow taste some.

Willow could not have become so STRONG on the hillside.

One day Willow was showing Victoria the gap left by her first two baby teeth coming out right in the front of her mouth, when the shepherd and Mist arrived with the trailer. It was time to go home.

Willow said goodbye to Victoria.

The trailer ride back seemed to last forever. When the ramp was lowered all the lambs rushed out. Willow jumped for joy.

Willow remembered every step of the way back…

…to the place where she had been born just over a year ago. And there was her mother – not alone – but with Willow's new brother and sister.